THE JOKE'S ON YOU, BATMAN!

Adapted by R. J. Cregg
Illustrated by Patrick Spaziante
Based on the screenplay *Monster Mayhem* written by Heath Corson
Batman created by Bob Kane with Bill Finger

Simon Spotlight
New York London Toronto Sydney New Delhi

Based on the screenplay by Heath Corson

SIMON SPOTLIGHT
An imprint of Simon & Schuster Children's Publishing Division
1230 Avenue of the Americas, New York, New York 10020
This Simon Spotlight paperback edition December 2016
All rights reserved, including the right of reproduction in whole or in part in any form.
SIMON SPOTLIGHT and colophon are registered trademarks of Simon & Schuster, Inc.
For information about special discounts for bulk purchases, please contact Simon & Schuster Special Sales
at 1-866-506-1949 or business@simonandschuster.com.
Manufactured in the United States of America 1116 LAK
10 9 8 7 6 5 4 3 2 1
ISBN 978-1-4814-7727-7
ISBN 978-1-4814-7728-4 (eBook)

Tonight, Bruce Wayne is at Gotham City's history museum. He has traded his Batsuit for a tuxedo as high society gathers to celebrate a new addition to the museum, the Inca Rose Stone. With the recent crime spree, Bruce and his friends, Cyborg, Dick Grayson, and Oliver Queen, are expecting trouble.

"There are a lot of people who made this amazing discovery happen," says the master of ceremonies. "But Cyborg was the one who actually found the Inca Rose Stone." The crowd applauds the hero. "I also wanted to extend a big thank-you to—"

"Me!" interrupts the Joker as he pushes the man aside. "Howdy, Gotham City! Miss me?"

The crowd gasps at the super-villain. Bruce, Dick, and Oliver slip out of the crowd to change into their super suits.

"I don't want any trouble," the Joker says. "But, my friend here—he *loves* trouble!" With a monstrous roar, one of the museum's dinosaur sculptures comes to life!

The dinosaur turns out to be the infamous shapeshifter Clayface! This is just the kind of trouble Batman was expecting. He and his friends, Nightwing, Green Arrow, and Cyborg, return to the fray and spring into action.

"You're going extinct, lizard breath!" says Cyborg as he fires his lasers at Clayface.

As the heroes hunt down Clayface, the Joker steals the Inca Rose Stone. "Ooo! What a belt buckle you'd make. It's a shame I have other plans for you. HAHAHAHA!" he laughs.

The heroes chase the villains out to the street, but suddenly Batman's Batcycle malfunctions.

"It must be a computer virus," says Batman.

Across town Cyborg's inner computer has also been infected by the Joker's Digital Laughing Virus. As he laughs helplessly, Clayface and the rest of the Joker's gang take him away.

At the Batcave the heroes regroup with Red Robin, just as the Joker's face appears on every screen in the city. "As you can see," says the Joker. "My Digital Laughing Virus has affected every piece of technology . . . which makes me King of Gotham City."

"We're going to have to do this the old-fashioned way," says Batman, coming up with a plan.

Batman breaks into the Joker's headquarters to fight him, but first he overhears the Joker talking to himself.

"It's like Christmas morning, except I'm waiting for world domination!" says the Joker.

He isn't just taking over Gotham City, Batman realizes. *He's going to use the Inca Rose Stone to transmit his virus to the entire world!*

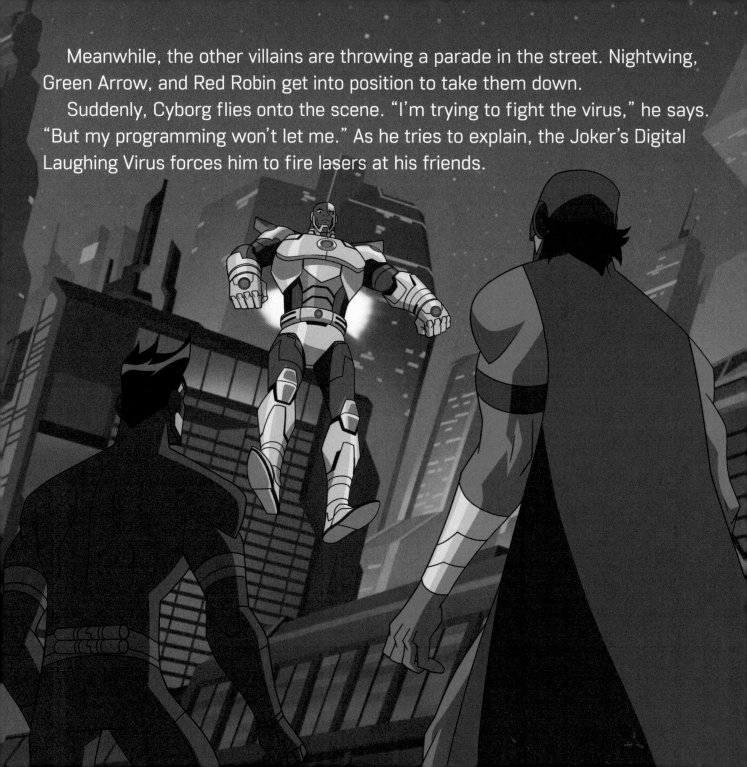

Meanwhile, the other villains are throwing a parade in the street. Nightwing, Green Arrow, and Red Robin get into position to take them down.

Suddenly, Cyborg flies onto the scene. "I'm trying to fight the virus," he says. "But my programming won't let me." As he tries to explain, the Joker's Digital Laughing Virus forces him to fire lasers at his friends.

Inside the Joker's headquarters, Batman finds the virus on the Joker's computer and enters a virtual reality program to destroy it. The virus isn't going down without a fight though: Thousands of virtual Jokers appear in the program, ready to battle. Batman throws a punch at the nearest Joker, but misses.

"It's not going to be that easy," says the Joker's virus. "You're in my world now, and I like things a little crazy."

Luckily Batman knows his way around a computer. He creates a virtual T-rex to battle the virus. With every punch, kick, and laser blast, he infects the virtual Jokers with his own counterprogramming.

"Looks like your virus caught a virus," Batman says.

"Come on! That's cheating," complains the last Joker as it's deleted. "What a way to go!"

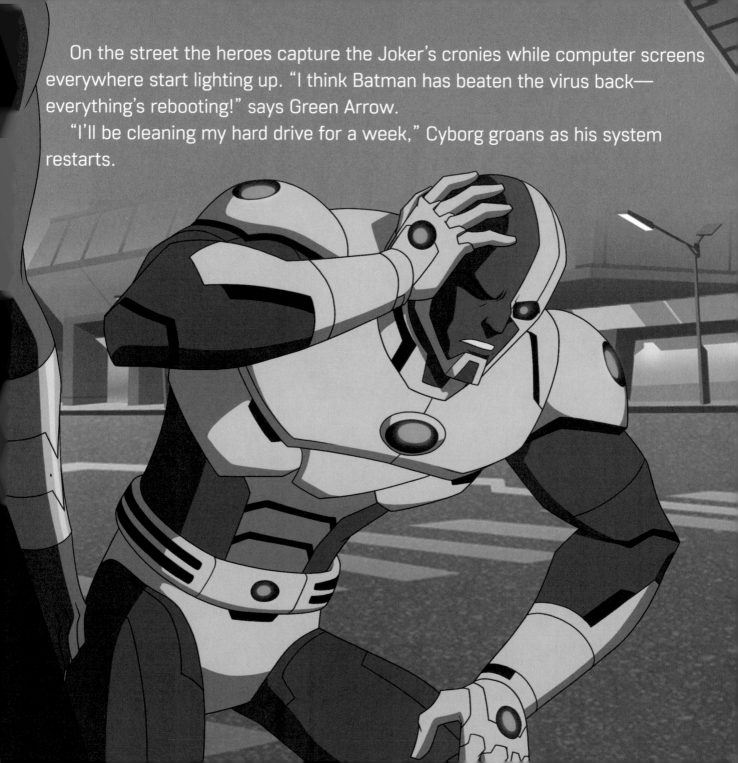

On the street the heroes capture the Joker's cronies while computer screens everywhere start lighting up. "I think Batman has beaten the virus back— everything's rebooting!" says Green Arrow.

"I'll be cleaning my hard drive for a week," Cyborg groans as his system restarts.

Suddenly the Joker broadcasts again. "Did you really think I would transmit my Digital Laughing Virus from only one location? Suckers!" He bursts onto the street in his Joker Mech.

"We're going to need tech to take that thing down," says Nightwing.

"Follow me," says Batman, joining his friends on the street.

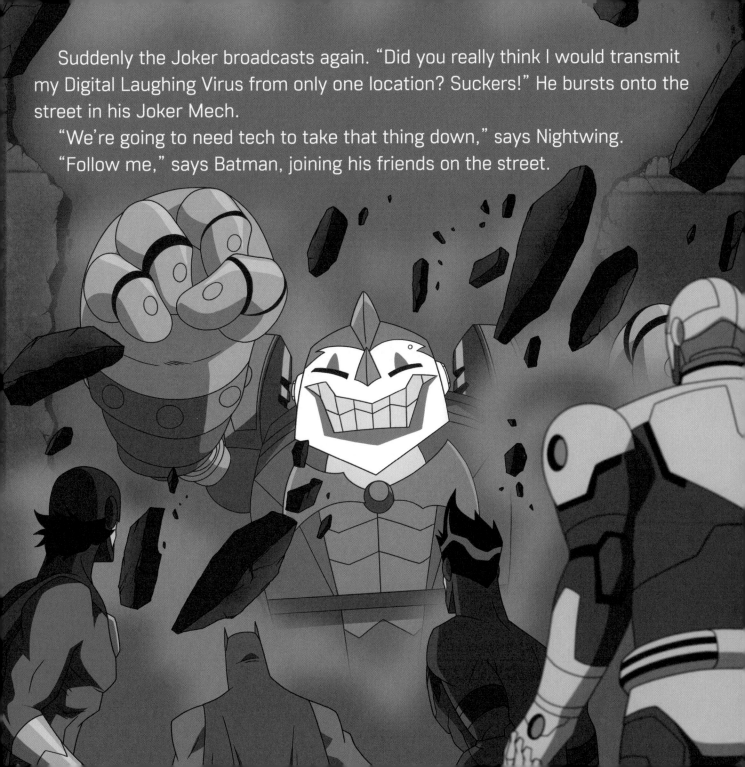

"I never thought I'd say this, but thank goodness for the history museum!" says Red Robin as he and Nightwing speed off on their borrowed World War II motorcycles. Older equipment, like their bikes, doesn't have computers, so the Joker's Digital Laughing Virus didn't affect them!

Green Arrow drives a tank. He brings down the Joker Mech with one shot. *BAM!*

But the Joker escapes again, flying away in his jet-powered stealth suit—he can still unleash his virus on the world!

"The Joker needs a boosted quantum computer to transmit the virus worldwide," Batman says as he trails the villain in an old fighter plane. "The only person with such a computer is—Cyborg!"

Cyborg scans his arm. Batman is right! The Joker put the Inca Rose Stone in Cyborg's arm. With the power generated by the stone, the Joker can use the hero's boosted quantum computer to send his virus anywhere.

FOREIGN OBJECT IDENTIFIED

"You're going to have to attach the stone to the Joker's suit," Batman tells Cyborg. "Attach it to the central core, and that should be enough to overload the suit's central computer and shut down the virus forever."

"Here goes everything!" Cyborg says as he punches the stone directly into the central core of the Joker's stealth suit.

The Joker falls out of the sky and into the river as his suit short-circuits. The city is saved!

"Good night, Gotham City!" says Clayface as he and the Joker's other henchmen are loaded into a police van.

"Quick selfie?" asks a boy, holding up his cell phone.

Now that the danger has passed, the heroes gather on a rooftop.
"We combed the bay. No sign of the Joker," says Nightwing.
  "He'll be back," says Batman.
  "We'll be here when he is," says Green Arrow. "I can always count on Gotham City for a thrill."

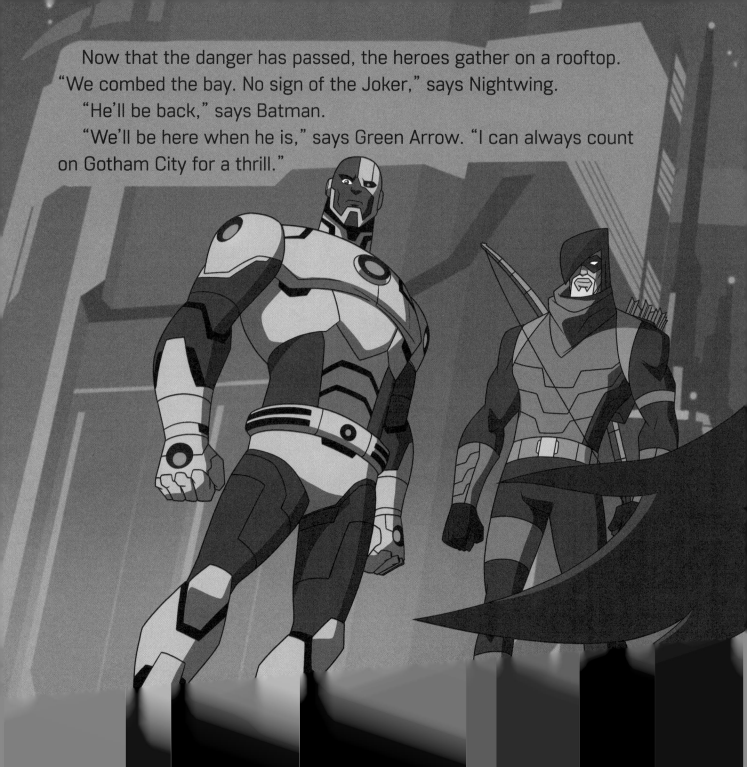

On the other side of the river, the Joker walks away dripping wet. "I should be King of the World right now," he says. "Oh well. Maybe I'll open a pizza joint and call it Giggles! Hahahaha! I like the sound of that."

One way or another, the Joker always gets the last laugh.